Paddy's Recess Adventures at Hilltop School

by Sean Rooney

Strategic Book Publishing and Rights Co.

Strategic Book Publishing and Rights Co., LLC
USA | Singapore
www.sbpra.com

For information about special discounts for bulk purchases, please contact Strategic Book Publishing and Rights Co., LLC. Special Sales, at bookorder@sbpra.net.

ISBN: 978-1-68181-986-0

Welcome to the second book of the Hilltop School Series. The first book of the series starred a muskrat named Paddy who drove a bright yellow wheelchair with lime green racing stripes. Paddy has cerebral palsy. In the first book, he had to move from Tennessee to South Carolina because his dad changed jobs. On his journey he ran into a little bit of trouble with a bully named Luke the skunk. However, his new friend Austin the rabbit came to save him.

Even though Paddy is different on the outside,

He is very thoughtful and cares about his friends.

Paddy and Luke will forever make memories

Because of all the time they will spend together

Once upon a time at Hilltop School, before Paddy the muskrat came to town, Luke the skunk and Austin the rabbit were inseparable. They went swimming together, went to soccer games together, and they had sleepovers together. They did everything together. When Paddy came to their school, things changed. This was the first time that Luke had seen someone in a wheelchair, and he wasn't sure how he felt about Paddy.

Luke the skunk saw how Paddy and Austin had become good friends, and he felt pushed aside. Luke was jealous because he missed playing with just Austin. Luke became a bully towards Paddy.

One day Luke called his friends Will, Kale, Gabriella, and Carrie over. They were skunks too and they were part of his skunk gang. Luke whispered to them, "We're going to start a secret club! Since it's my club and I make the rules, I'm making it only skunks allowed!"

"Why?" they asked. "Well skunks are just better. Plus, Paddy and Austin have become such good friends—Austin sort of left us," said Luke. They agreed to Luke's rules because they didn't want to be kicked out.

Luke said, "Follow me. I found a tree that would be perfect for our club in the back of the school yard!" Luke's skunk gang followed behind him. They found the peach tree with several ripe fruits on it. The peach tree had a hole in it that was big enough to store their snacks and play in.

"This is where the Secret Peach Tree Recess Club is going to be," Luke said. He reached into his fur coat and pulled out a little brown trumpet. "See this?" he asked in a commanding voice. "It's very important that when you hear me blow this trumpet that you come right away. It's a call to get together. If anyone's not here by the third time I blow the horn, you're automatically out!" he snorted.

"But that's not fair!" they cried.

"Do you want to be in this club or not?" Luke asked them. "And this rule is the most important one. Don't tell anyone about this! We have to keep this club only skunks."

"Alright," they all slowly agreed. The bell rang for recess to end. Everyone filed back into their classrooms.

One of Luke's skunk friends, Will, was in Paddy and Austin's class. Mrs. Huggins was their teacher. She had a furry red carpet where everyone sat for the after-recess discussion and story time.

Mrs. Huggins said, "Will, you're up first. What was your favorite part of recess today?"

"We started our own club!" he blurted out with excitement.

"A new club?" Paddy whispered to Austin. "I wonder if we can join."

"We'll have to find out where it is," Austin said excitedly.

"Where does your club meet?" Mrs. Huggins asked Will. Paddy and Austin leaned in to listen for where it was. Will remembered that Luke said not to tell, but he knew Mrs. Huggins didn't allow people to keep secrets.

"In a tree by the school yard," Will said.

"That sounds fun," said Mrs. Huggins. "Thank you for sharing."

The next day at recess, Paddy and Austin followed Will and noticed where the special club was located. They found the tree that Will was talking about, and knocked on the tree.

"What do you want?" Luke asked in a snotty voice. Then he saw who it was. Luke was in complete shock when he saw them.

"Hi," they said in very friendly voices. "We just heard about this club and we wondered if we could become members."

"Hold on," Luke answered in a mean voice. He turned back inside the tree. "What are they doing here?" Luke demanded. "How did they find out about our hiding spot?"

"Oh no! I told Mrs. Huggins about the peach tree and they must have followed me here!" Will said.

"I told you not to tell! Now look what you've done!" Luke said to him in a threatening voice. "Why couldn't you just have kept quiet?"

"Because Mrs. Huggins doesn't let us do that. We have to come up with something," Will said.

"What's the big deal with having them join?" Gabriella asked. "It's not going to hurt anything."

Luke looked at her angrily and said, "Because, remember what I said?"

Paddy and Austin leaned in to listen because they were curious about what they were saying.

"They're not skunks, and skunks are the best animals. Plus, Austin left us to be friends with Paddy."

Paddy and Austin didn't think that was very nice, so they went back to the playground.

The next day at recess, Luke blew the trumpet for his club members to meet at the tree. Carrie didn't realize Luke was blowing the trumpet until after the noise stopped, so she didn't get there on time.

"Where is Carrie?" Luke asked the other club members.

"I'm here!" Carrie said as she ran up. "I didn't hear the trumpet until the last blow because I was on the swings.

"Sorry," Luke said, "but you know the rules. You're no longer a part of this club. And also Will, because you let it slip yesterday, you have to leave, too."

Gabriella quickly spoke up. "If you can't make an exception for him since he had to tell his teacher, then that's not fair. That's just one of his teacher's rules. I'm quitting!"

After Gabriella left, Luke started eating his mom's famous red velvet muffins. He was going to offer a muffin to Kale, but then he noticed that Kale didn't join him in the tree. When Luke found Kale in the schoolyard, Luke asked, "Why aren't you in the tree?

the tree."

Kale said, "You know what, Luke? You're too bossy, and you're not making this club any fun for anyone but yourself. So I'm quitting, too." Kale scurried back to the other animals that were playing freeze tag.

Luke watched sadly as his former club members were having fun with the other animals. Paddy got tagged by someone and did the best he could to stay frozen, but when he noticed Luke snacking on a muffin looking very sad, he drove his bright yellow wheelchair with lime green racing stripes towards the tree.

Lauren the skunk said, "You're frozen! Where are you going?"

"You guys play without me. There's something I have to do right now," said Paddy.

Once Paddy got there, he asked, "Hey Luke, what are you doing here all by yourself? Why don't you come and join our game of freeze tag?"

"Why are you letting me join after I was so rude to you?" Luke asked sadly.

"Because," Paddy answered. "I know how it feels to be left out."

Luke said, "I'm sorry for the mean things I've done to you. I am going to be nicer from now on."

"Okay," Paddy said. "Enough with this sorry stuff. Just come on and play! It'll be fun!"

Luke laughed, put his muffins back in his lunch box, and followed Paddy to join his friends, both skunks and other animals. Luke knew inside that Paddy would always be different, but being different made him a special friend. Luke and Austin would always be Paddy's friends. He would never bully Paddy again.

The End.

9 781681 819860